Baby Bruise
Copyright © 2023/2024 Danielle Chelosky
Cover design by Danielle Chelosky
Layout by Ira Rat

This is a work of fiction. Names, characters, businesses, places, events, locales, and incidents are either the products of the author's imagination or used in a fictitious manner. Any resemblance to actual persons, living or dead, or actual events is purely coincidental.

This book may not be reproduced in whole or in part, except for the inclusion of brief quotations in a review, without permission in writing from the author or publisher. No part of this publication may be reproduced, stored in or introduced into retrieval system, or transmitted, in any form, or by any means (electronic, mechanical, photocopying, recording, or otherwise), without prior permission of the publisher.

Requests for permission should be directed to filthylootpress@gmail.com

FIRST EDITION

baby bruise
danielle chelosky

TALENTED PERVERTS

filthyloot.com

ALSO BY DANIELLE CHELOSKY

Pregaming Grief
show me your face
Cheat

1.
Exorcism

I sat in the bath, lips against my knee, teeth absentmindedly sucking skin, mind filled with unrequited love. A week earlier, my crush, Matt, admitted his feelings shortly before displaying his true colors, letting my texts go unanswered and hiding from me in the hallways. Every time I went near my phone I hallucinated his call, the echo of a ring in my brain when there was only silence.

It was all my fault. I invested myself too deeply. Or was it too early? Pages of poems penned with an unstable hand. I made the mistake of giving away my words, hoping the affection would be appreciated while knowing it wouldn't. He was insecure—despite his popularity and lead role in every play, he never lived up to his divorced parents' expectations. His mother was a therapist who avoided his anguish and her contribution to it, and his father was an English professor whose extracurricular concerns rarely involved anything beyond fictional characters. He divulged all this via text at three a.m. after we'd only known each other a few days. We went over his lines in the cafeteria when the gaps between our classes lined up. We read and reread sections he highlighted, dancing around heavy discussions from the night before. Some conversations were meant only for the dark. I knew he was my first love by the way every new sensation settled in me, like the effects of a drug. Love molded time into unprecedented shapes, our days long and strangely blissful, brimming with possibility. Love was an amphetamine driving me to finally clean my room after a mountain range of clothes formed along the river of trash overflowing the bin during a deep depression. But love was fragile and shattered when I dropped it. He hid from me like he hid from his parents.

A soft knock on the window interrupted my thoughts. I heard the violent vibration all the way from the bathroom. I paused, my mouth still busy on my leg. A second knock lifted me from the lukewarm water. Dripping, I drained the tub and stepped onto the mat. I wrapped myself in my pink towel. After tiptoeing to my bedroom I flinched at the sight in my window: Vivian, waving and smiling frantically. It took me a moment to realize the pitter-patter came from the raindrops outside, to which Vivian seemed impervious. She held a water bottle of amber liquid in her hand. I could smell the whiskey from where I stood as I removed the frame and twisted the knob before sliding the window open. I gripped her wrist until she tumbled in. She went right for the closet and picked out my purple slip, raising her eyebrows.

"It's thirty degrees out," I said.

She unbuttoned her jacket to reveal a strapless pink top with a white skirt and knee socks hugging her legs. "And?" she said.

Vivian was weary of my tireless lamentations. I only told her about Matt after he stopped talking to me; the secrecy made it special. It wasn't just a high school romance, wasn't about status or drama, wasn't one relationship in a deluge of teenage flings. We understood each other. It was hard to explain to Vivian, who preferred sacrilege over sacredness. Besides, she never liked him anyway; she often complained about how he always showed off in class, a teacher's pet striding the halls with an obnoxious sense of purpose. But she didn't know him like I did, how weak he was beneath the mask. No one knew it was all a façade, that he wasn't as confident as he pretended to be, always an actor playing a part.

I didn't know how I ended up in the purple slip, my sneakers thumping against the sidewalk through my neighborhood. I no longer had a reason to say no. Matt was slipping through my fingers. I couldn't be alone. I left my window open for when I got home but only slightly ajar, invisible to the eyes of passersby. The icy air cut through the silk straight to the skin like a blade. Birds circled in the drizzly night sky. For a moment I wanted to kill myself, to find a speeding car to toss my body in front of—if only for the possibility of reincarnation with wings and a new sense of direction.

"I have my fake ID," Vivian said as we approached the gas station. Two cars were parked at the pumps, men leaning against their trunks while filling their tanks. "We're gonna get a case of beer. There's a party on Lunar. It'll be a long walk. Unless we hitchhike…"

She smiled to sell the suicide mission. I gestured toward the main road and its glaring emptiness. She rolled her eyes, and I rolled mine back and I thought we could go on forever until they popped out of their sockets and rolled down the road.

Whenever I confessed to sneaking out, my therapist told me I was rebelling against my father, who left before I was born. I would've appreciated this fallacy had it served as an excuse; instead, it was her way of blaming me, of acting like I was a sinner who needed to be put on the right path. I stopped seeing therapists.

In chemistry class, I got paired up with a kid named Aiden. We talked about our mutual hatred for the course. The experiment Aiden and I were tasked with was quick and easy, the only kind I could handle. We dropped dry ice in a flask of boiling water and a stream of fog emerged, a grey outpouring so thick I wanted to grab it, though I knew it was only vapor.

"I'm surprised you're cool," Aiden said as we stashed our materials and washed our hands. I accepted his backhanded compliment with ambivalence. "You're strange, always walking around with earbuds in and whispering to yourself."

It was just like me to wear my morbidity on my sleeve. I never thought about how I appeared to others; in the hallways, I savored the minutes between classes as opportunities to immerse myself in music. I often let the words take shape in my mouth, moving my lips without releasing sound. I tried to stop myself after Aiden pointed this out but always found myself surrounded by lyrics, subconsciously exorcised. I listened to songs from my childhood. My mom only listened to *Rumours* by Fleetwood Mac for years, and I had thought they were the only band in the world. She blasted the CD in the car, windows rolled down, ashing her cigarette on the street, singing along so loud as if trying to reach my dad, wherever he was. Eventually, she gave up and never put them on again.

At the convenience store, the fluorescent lights glowed white, offering the atmosphere of a hospital. I picked up a Kit Kat bar as Vivian opened the fridge and lugged a pack of Corona to the counter. The cashier, a middle-aged Indian man, stared at her vacantly. "ID?"

She reached into her tiny pink purse. Her eyes widened as she rummaged. She turned and looked at me. We stepped away from the counter. "I think

I left my wallet at mine," she whispered to me.

"I obviously can't show him my ID," I whispered back.

We sighed in unison. Our exhales mingled with the sound of the bell chiming above the doors, an amorphous enchantment ringing through the air. Vivian stood in my peripheral vision as my eyes locked with the stranger's as he entered. His gaze struck me with a sense of familiarity and the pang of a thrill. I barely felt my lips unfurling into a smile but noticed when his did the same, reflecting mine. Above anything, I felt a cosmic closeness, as if we inhabited the same secret world. Everything else came after, like the fact he looked twice my age, like the look of his sooty wifebeater, his greasy brown hair, the look of his unshaven, aged face.

"Ladies, are you going to show me ID or what?" the cashier said, his voice disrupting the moment.

Vivian looked worried. My smile faded to a frown. Suddenly, the stranger approached the cashier, leafing through his wallet. "My bad, Jay," he said, handing him a twenty. "My nieces are in town. I sent them in to pick this up for me. Forgot they weren't old enough. Damn alcohol laws."

Another smile. I felt it this time—my lips spread as far as they could until my face almost hurt. I saw it in Vivian, too, except her eyebrows knit together, and she glanced at me skeptically. I searched for a similar feeling in myself—reluctance, confusion, something along those lines—but found nothing.

"Oh, let me get a pack of Camel Blues, too," said the stranger.

Jay pulled the pack from the cigarette wall and set it on the counter. I timidly slid my Kit Kat beside it, turning my head toward the stranger as a way of asking. "This, too," he told Jay.

Outside the gas station, Vivian and I stalled as the stranger plucked a cigarette from his pack and lit it. "We could use a ride," I blurted to him.

"Actually, we're fine," Vivian assured him, shooting me another glance.

"Your friend is right," the stranger said to me.

"You shouldn't ask strangers for rides. But where you headed?"

Vivian perked up at that—as if his acknowledgment of himself as a stranger meant he no longer was one. "Lunar Road," she replied.

He laughed, smoke pouring from the void of his mouth. "What're you girls up to?" he asked. Vivian's lips parted to respond, but before she could, he said, "You know what, I don't want to know."

He walked to an old car parked at the pump. It looked like he drove it right out of the '90s, the emerald body with every edge rectangular, the kind of car I imagined serial killers drove. I ran to the passenger door and slumped onto the soft seat, kicking my feet up on the dashboard. He put the beers in the backseat next to Vivian. We exchanged curious looks in the rearview mirror. "I'm Otto," the stranger said as he inserted the keys into the ignition. "And you two are…?"

"I'm Lavender," Vivian said.

I giggled under my breath. "I'm February," I said. It was March.

Otto sighed and put the car in drive. "Whatever you ladies say."

Vivian fidgeted with the seatbelt, a clumsy clashing of metal. "That doesn't work," Otto said as he sharply turned, sending Vivian flying across the cushions. "Better hold on tight."

He only cracked the window slightly, a sliver of the outside for his smoke to drift into. Without looking, he clicked a button. I heard the winding and unwinding of a cassette tape before a gentle acoustic guitar echoed through the car, the quality so poor it sounded miles away yet clearly full of emotion. It was a short ride on the main road. We soared through streaks of green lights, unstoppable.

He pointed to the purple blob on my knee. "You've got a baby bruise," he said. I hadn't noticed it forming all those nights in the bathtub, my mouth mindlessly on my leg, wondering when someone else's tongue and teeth would birth new colors on my skin.

"You can call me that if you want," I said. He didn't look at me, just smirked and shook his head.

On Lunar, he parked in front of the driveway of a tan ranch-style home with all its lights on. "Don't do drugs," he said. "Or do them. I don't care. Have a good night, Lavender and Baby Bruise."

He unlocked the doors and Vivian hopped out. I lingered for a moment, thinking of a question to ask, a request to stay in touch, but no words felt right, so I said nothing and slipped out. The car skidded into the night like it was never there, as if we'd teleported.

Polly slouched on the garish purple loveseat, her head tilted as she drained a beer. I sank into the ratty plaid couch. The beige walls were decorated with holes. Glass littered the floor; teens laughed and cried as blood gushed from their heels. For the third time, Polly lit a cigarette, took a few puffs, then handed it off to a stranger passing by.

"Why do you keep doing that?" I asked.

"The first few sips of a cigarette are beautiful,"

she said. "The rest are rotten."

Polly named herself after the Nirvana song. No one knew her real name. I reluctantly drank red wine from a Solo cup. I'd only ever been buzzed before, modestly sipping beer over the course of a night, mostly just to have something to hold. Sixteen and still yet to experience intoxication. I felt like a loser, but I'd been warned. My mom sent my brother to Arizona for the addiction he inherited. Who knows what had been passed down to me? It baffled me how a liquid or a little pill could hypnotize someone into wanting more and more, how such a tiny thing could take away all control.

Witnessing the madness of the house party, I thought it'd be a relief to relinquish control. I was tired of being in my head, of watching everything happen instead of being a part of it. The guitars coming from Otto's speakers still reverberated through my mind. I thought *Otto Otto Otto*, a wonderfully symmetrical name, almost musical. The same number of letters as *Matt*, yet infinitely more poetic and rare. Otto was one of a kind, while the world was overpopulated with Matts.

A trapdoor: I fell into the present when Matt emerged from the kitchen, materializing before me just like that. I'd summoned him by thinking his name, an accidental incantation.

"Are you OK?" Polly said, but I didn't hear her. Like how stars die but we still see their glow for years after, it took a while for her question to reach me, as if I was hidden behind an intergalactic barrier.

The universe played a trick on me—how humiliating. For the first time in a week, I felt free of his grip, no longer weighed down by his vague rejection. Now here he was, the face of endless punishment. I chugged the rest of the wine, tilting my head to keep our eyes from meeting. But once the bitter liquid slid down my throat, his eyes were the first thing I saw—only a flash before his brown irises shifted awkwardly away. So that was my answer, his rejection finally taking shape.

Drunk and dangerous, Vivian grabbed my

hand and led me to the kitchen. The floor was a labyrinth of purple tiles stained with dirt from everyone's shoes. She plucked a Corona from the fridge and handed it to me. As I reached for the bottle, she smirked and let it go, glass shattering at our feet, which were now swimming in the sticky pool. My frown had no effect on her evil ecstasy. I didn't know what to do, so I turned to the bounty of bottles on the marble island and took a huge swig of vodka: immediate flashback to childhood and my mom force-feeding me pungent medicine, then the memory of nail polish remover erasing a vibrant pink.

I understood then the hold alcohol had over people. A surge of disgust shot through me like a spirit—I was ready to be exorcised and wanted to give myself over to this ghost. I stumbled to the living room, where an abandoned table held the remains of a beer pong game. Bud Lite puddled on the wood among a pile of toppled Solo cups. A chandelier lit everything a sinister orange. Vivian snuck up behind me as I gawked at a shitty Pollock knockoff hung slightly off-kilter on the wall.

Summoning saliva from the back of my throat, I aimed for the center like a bullseye. My spit landed on a spot of red paint, and Vivian shrieked so loud I almost didn't hear the screams in the other room. Bodies rushed toward the front door as everyone scrambled to escape. Vivian grabbed my hand and we were in flight, some mystical force keeping us upright as we staggered along through the throng.

We saw Polly on the sidewalk, hunched over to catch her breath. "What's going on?" Vivian asked.

"Someone yelled something about a gun," she said. "I don't think it's true, though. Lily probably just wanted to clear the house. Always works."

Vivian and I laughed. We kept running, the shared superpower of invincibility granted by the poison in our veins. Polly ran with us. The world was massive in this moment, the suburban streets desolate and paved for our misadventures. I watched myself from afar, saw my life finally begin. Polly lit a cigarette and took a few puffs before passing it to me. I slipped it between my fingers, slid it into my mouth, and inhaled.

2.
One-Time Killer

For a while, I only saw Otto in dreams. I was always walking along the main road when his car pulled up beside me. As soon as I slid in the passenger seat, he'd speed off and I'd wake up. I dreamt of drifting through the hallways at school and turning a corner to see Otto waiting on a windowsill for me.

I frequently snuck out at night and went to the

gas station, hoping to find him. Each time I placed my Kit Kat on the counter, Jay joked, "Another late-night snack?" I'd sit on the curb for half an hour before giving up and going home, where at least I knew I'd see Otto in my subconscious.

As my connection with Otto dissolved, my heartbreak over Matt resurfaced. His play—a production of Arthur Miller's *The Crucible*—was approaching and he was playing John Proctor, a fittingly cruel role. Vivian suggested we attend just to throw tomatoes. While I appreciated her enthusiasm, I would much rather have been anywhere else than in a room with him. He was already on a pedestal in my heart—I didn't need to see him on a stage reveling in all the attention and admiration, the only things he seemed to care about, an obvious way to make up for the lack of love from his parents. But who knows? I sure as hell wasn't a therapist.

I knew it wasn't Matt I loved, but rather the flash of requited affection. The familial turmoil he revealed, the routine of practicing lines together.

Love gave life a beautiful rhythm—without it, everything returned to nonsense as usual. How could I go back to who I was? I didn't know that person anymore. *Did I ever?* Matt made me feel seen—something I'd never felt but always yearned for—then ran away, leaving me worse than if he'd never seen me at all.

None of this should've mattered. A year from now, I'd be getting ready to leave this life behind for a new town in a new state for college. Still, I was paranoid something would get in my way. I couldn't imagine escaping the place I grew up. It was all I ever wanted, and now it was so close I assumed it would collapse at any moment. Anything could happen in a year. I submitted applications and stared at brochures adorned with smiling students on sprawling lawns leading to castles—it looked too good to be true.

That night at the party, Vivian flirted with Simon, a high school dropout from a neighboring town. He claimed to be eighteen—only a couple years older than us—but I suspected he was in his mid-twenties (who was I to judge, though, with my dreams of Otto?). The next weekend, Simon's blue Mustang rumbled into my neighborhood. I wanted to shush the car, but I knew my mom was already deep in Twisted Tea sleep. Climbing out of my window had become a familiar routine, nearly second nature. Clad in my favorite strapless top, shortest skirt, and brand-new bomber jacket, I casually crossed the lawn and hopped into the backseat. Simon obnoxiously revved his engine before speeding past the stop sign at the end of the block. I couldn't see him from where I sat, only the reflection of his eyes in the rearview mirror. He twisted a knob, turning the music louder as the walls vibrated to the beat.

Simon whispered, and Vivian snickered, but I couldn't hear what he said over the booming bass. As we cruised toward an unknown destination, Vivian turned and handed me a tiny plastic bottle. I hesitantly took it, examining the label: tequila. Before I could reply, Vivian held up a half-empty Sprite. "Need a chaser?"

I accepted it without thinking, letting nothing get in my way. I wanted to be impulsive like I'd been that night at the house party. I drained the bottle in one gulp and chased it with the Sprite. There it was again: that rush, that invincibility. Suddenly, Simon's recklessness filled me with delight, the blaring music a blanket of comfort in the chaos. It was the most at home I'd ever felt—in a stranger's speeding car, liquor soaring through my bloodstream.

The sky glowed purple through the tinted glass, the stars shadowy in their messy constellations. When Simon rolled down the windows, Vivian screamed and laughed. I quietly giggled, too, keeping my amusement to myself. The wind twisted our hair into knots that would keep us tied up for hours the next day. As Simon started rolling up the window on Vivian's outstretched arm, she screamed again.

Simon cruised into the cul-de-sac, braking so hard I almost slammed into his seat. "Alright," he said. "We're here."

To my right, a worn house flickered with thrill. Overlapping voices swirled through the air as vaguely familiar melodies spilled from a boombox. We stumbled out of the car, still giggling and slightly dizzy. Simon led the way to the front door, which he pushed open like he owned the place. For all I knew, he did.

I didn't recognize anyone. Vivian and Simon disappeared up the spiral staircase. Left alone, I wandered to the kitchen and poured vodka into a Solo cup. A boy asked me if I was a freshman. "I'm a senior," I lied, sipping my way back to that beloved state of invigoration. I knew it was within reach, I just needed a little more, a little more. The boy—who introduced himself as Leo—found it strange I was a senior because he'd never seen me around. When he named a school in another district, I considered clarifying but instead agreed, "Yeah, that's strange."

I should've carved my number into Otto's dashboard, I thought. I should've told him to meet me at the gas station. I felt frustrated, confused, drunk. I felt there had to be more to this night and this stupid party, but Vivian left me alone, lingering with my thoughts of the other weekend. Where was the excitement I'd just felt in the car? Maybe in another shot of tequila, I considered as I poured one. I tilted my head toward the sky, determined to find the answer.

"Want to have a cigarette?" Leo asked.

"Sure, why not," I said, following him to the back porch where some talked and smoked while others sat on laps, kissing.

Leo pulled a pack of Camel Blues from his varsity jacket. I smiled, taking one between my lips. He flicked his lighter and my cigarette hovered above the flame. I watched the ember burn as he lit his own. "I know you don't go to Lincoln," he said.

"You caught me," I replied.

"It's cool," he said. "I like a little mystery."

I rolled my eyes. Boys were so easy. They liked a challenge. They wanted to feel like detectives cracking open a case. They always thought there was some big secret waiting to be revealed. Little did he know there was nothing to discover.

When I didn't respond, he asked, "Want to know a secret?"

I nodded, exhaling smoke.

"This is Dave's party," he explained. "Dave is a CODA and he throws parties every weekend while his parents are asleep upstairs."

My eyes grew wide. I thought of Vivian and Simon tossing each other around on a creaky bed as a pair of parents slumbered unaware on the other side of the wall. "Wow," I said. "Is Dave your friend?"

Leo shook his head. "No one is Dave's friend," he said. "Dave's a trainwreck. He's gone to juvie twice and been suspended more times than anyone can count. Throwing textbooks at teachers, stabbing classmates with pencils, sneaking into the girls' bathroom to write on the stalls—you name it."

"Well, I don't feel so great here anymore," I

said.

"That's the thing," he continued. "He always acts normal at these parties. Like they're his one safe space, and he only has fun when he's drunk and thinks everybody loves him."

The door slid open and Vivian's voice rang out: "Let's do shots!" Before I could react, she grabbed me by the wrist and dragged me back in the house to the kitchen. Déjà vu struck as the liquor disappeared down my throat again, an action as natural as breathing or eating. My wrist still suffocated in Vivian's grip as she led me to the living room. A chandelier blasted white light onto wallpaper ripped at the bottom like a cat had scratched at it to reveal what lay hidden underneath. As a baby, I made the walls of our house a canvas for my crayons until my mom discovered my doodles and shouted. All I wanted was a playground house, a place with no rules.

The living room had no furniture, but the indented carpet indicated a table was once there, like the chalk outline of a body nowhere to be found. A group sat in a circle where the table had been, candles between each person and a bottle spinning in the center. Vivian nudged a blonde with her foot and the circle begrudgingly opened up. We entered the lopsided ring, and the bottle immediately pointed at Vivian. I saw the sparkle in her eyes and the smirk lighting her face. I wondered where Simon was. The bottle spun and Leo joined the circle, his eyes observing me curiously. I nervously looked away. He sat across from us as the bottle slowed then pointed right at him. I dug my nails into my thighs. I didn't know why I felt jealous. I hadn't spent enough time with Leo to catch feelings, yet I instinctively inflicted pain on myself to stay safe.

They leaned in, creating an arch in the circle's center. But instead of a quick peck, the kiss went on. Everyone in the circle gasped and giggled as Vivian rested both hands on his shoulders to steady herself. It wasn't until glass shattered behind us that they finally broke apart. All heads shot back toward the noise. Simon stood beside a lamp on the floor, its bulb reduced to shards.

Vivian lurched forward for what I assumed was a hug—some sort of comfort or consolation, assurance it was nothing and he was everything—but he pushed her away. Not even that hard, but she was drunk enough for the shove to send her to the floor. I got up to help but the circle closed in before I could reach her. Everyone flocked in from other rooms to help her and ask if she was OK. Simon disappeared and Vivian was crying. I wondered how we were getting home. I wondered where we were, whether anyone here would've helped if I'd been pushed. People crowded around Vivian, asking her name. "Lavender," she answered. A sudden fire burned in my veins.

I retreated to the kitchen and took a jug of water from the fridge. "Her name isn't really Lavender, is it?" a boy asked me. His eyes were orange-brown, a warm honey.

"You'll have to ask her," I answered, my life renewed by a few gulps of water.

The boy smiled and held out his hand. "Dave," he said with the comical air of a businessman.

Wrapping my fingers around his, I found a tiny plastic bag waiting for me in his palm. Baffled, I kept shaking his hand then slid the bag into my bomber. "And you?"

"Oh, sorry," I said. "I'm February."

He burst out laughing. "Sure you are," he said. His smile was so sincere I couldn't picture him chucking a textbook at a teacher. Could those stories just be myths? He silently poured and downed a shot, winked at me, and walked away. I felt like the chosen one with this mysterious gift bestowed upon me.

Vivian stumbled over, tugging at my skirt like a child. "Can we go home?" she murmured.

Sighing, I looked out the front door at the empty spot where Simon's car sat earlier. "We have no way of getting home."

"Someone here can drive us," she said.

"Everyone's drunk."

She looked at the floor dejectedly. "What about Otto?"

"Otto?" I asked. "We have no way of reaching him."

"I have his number," she said.

"What? How?"

"His phone was just sitting on the backseat," she said. "So I opened it and texted myself."

I was amazed, irritated, and excited all at once. "Give me your phone," I demanded.

She pulled it from her purse and smacked it in my palm. Her battery was about to die so I dashed to her messages and found the conversation with Otto. They hadn't interacted aside from the single text she sent, which made me feel relieved but also worried he wouldn't pick up. I tapped his name and called the number.

Time stretched impossibly for the first three rings. Defeat had begun to settle in when—"Hello?" his gravelly voice answered, familiar and exhilarating.

"Otto?" I replied. "It's February," I continued, struggling to keep up with all my fake names.

"Baby Bruise—remember? I'm with Lavender, and we need a ride. Please."

He mumbled but I couldn't make out any words. He sounded exhausted and blindsided by the call. What did men like him do on Friday nights? "Where are you?" he groaned.

"Good question," I said, scanning the dying party. I found Dave trying to flush his puke in the bathroom like a dazed animal scrambling to cover its tracks. I asked him to tell me the address and the town we were in. He paused to pull himself together, then muttered the number and names. I repeated his slurred words into the phone.

"OK," Otto said. "I'll be there in fifteen."

Vivian's phone died before I could thank him. I handed it back and we sat on the front porch steps, waiting for the serial killer sedan to arrive.

"I didn't like Simon," Vivian confessed. "I was just bored."

"Do you like anyone?" I asked.

"No," she replied. "Everyone's boring."

Vivian had her first boyfriend in kindergarten. I swear she hadn't gone a day without one since. And it's not like she needed anyone—if anything, it was the opposite. They always depended on her, and she loved the power. I couldn't blame her, either. It must've felt intoxicating to have all those boys wrapped around her finger.

My drooping lids shot open at the sight of the distinctive emerald. To my right, Vivian cupped her chin in her palm, both eyes sealed shut. After shaking her awake, I heaved her into the backseat then sat shotgun beside Otto.

"How the hell'd you get my number?" he asked.

Looking back at sleeping Vivian sprawled across the backseat, I had the urge to mount Otto even though he was behind the wheel. Instead, I buckled myself in and said, "Don't worry about it," then directed him to Vivian's.

Otto was silent the rest of the way—no questions or cassettes, just the smoke from the Camel between his lips. I shook Vivian awake when we arrived at her place. After finding her key I unlocked the door then led her to the bedroom. I flipped the switch and the harsh yellow rays exposed piles of clothes flooding the floor, half-drunk coffee cups covering every surface, and an unmade bed. Collapsing onto the mattress, she uttered a groan I took as my cue to go. Before leaving, I plugged in her phone and waited for it to turn back on. Once it did, I sent myself Otto's number and deleted every trace of him from her phone. Just to be safe.

I buckled myself in and guided Otto to my house, though I would've preferred his. Trying to describe how I felt about him was like grasping for something that didn't exist. "You ladies should be more careful," he chimed in. "What if I'd been drinking? What if I wasn't around to pick you up?"

"I appreciate your concern," I said. "But we would've found a way. We always do."

He shook his head. "I could be a serial killer, for all you know."

"Are you?" I asked.

He took his eyes off the road to meet mine. "No," he said. After a pause, he added, "Just a one-time killer. Couldn't get into it. Wasn't my thing."

We laughed.

"I had a dream about you," I lied. If I'd been truthful, I would've said *a lot of dreams.*

This surprised him so much he shot through a stop sign. "Fuck," he sputtered, his foot scrambling for the brake. But it was too late. I saw how upset he was and let out a laugh. I didn't think men—especially older ones—got flustered like that. "What are you laughing at?" he snapped.

"You're like a little kid," I giggled.

"No, I'm not," he replied defensively. "I'm a man twice your age."

I wanted to ask him a stupid question—like if he thought I was pretty—but resisted, not wanting to seem childish. Then suddenly I felt sick, everything I'd consumed tonight rising up in the back of my throat. "Oh no," I uttered.

"Pulloverpulloverpulloverpullover."

He slammed the brakes and slid up to a curb. Tumbling out of the car just in time, I vomited right outside a small house that held a therapist's office, according to the sign on the lawn. The last thing I saw was Matt's last name carved in script before chunks of colorful muck shot out of me onto the sidewalk, Otto holding my hair from behind. A horror spread through me with such intensity it bordered on beauty. I wanted it to never end and I wanted it to end immediately.

"You done?" Otto asked the second I stopped, or maybe a few seconds after, my sense of time distorted.

"I think so," I said, gazing up into his sad eyes. He wiped my mouth with his shirt and we briefly looked at each other just like we did when we first met. He shuffled back over to the car.

Then, more silence. "What if there's nothing left inside me?" I accidentally asked aloud.

"What?" Otto questioned.

"Nothing," I said, ashamed.

"You just threw up the bad stuff," he said. "The good stuff's still in you. Like your organs and brains and stuff."

"My brain is bad," I said.

"Well," he sighed. "Drinking's just gonna make it worse. I'll tell you that much right now."

He parked in front of my house. I didn't know what to say. "Thank you," I offered. I wanted to ask him where he lived, what he did, who he was, if he wanted me and dreamt about me, too—but he looked frustrated, so I let it go. "Bye-bye, Baby Bruise," he said. He waited for me to climb through my window before driving off. I stumbled to the bathroom. Puking more in the toilet, I pretended Otto was still behind me, holding my hair back.

3.
Waiting Around To Die

In my favorite memory with Matt, we took a walk across the field, making our way down the hill to the middle school where his play rehearsals transpired. I'd offered to join after we went over lines together in the cafeteria, expecting he'd say no. Shattering my certainty, his face lit up as he led me out through the school's front doors into a world where our connection would finally materialize. I suppressed my urge to hold his hand. He untangled his earbuds and gave one to me. I inserted it in my right ear, and he put the other in his left. This was the closest we'd come to kissing, like we were hopelessly handcuffed.

The loud and clumsy music scraped my eardrums, but a smile held on my face as we trudged through the grass.

"Do you like Blink-182?" he asked.

"I've never heard of them," I said, embarrassed for being out of the know. But Matt never made me feel like I should be ashamed about anything. He was always so understanding and reassuring.

As the drums crashed and collapsed into vocals, I couldn't comprehend anyone enjoying this. I wondered what Matt saw in this band's sound. There had to be something I was missing. Then the man with the microphone said: *Because when I'm with you, there's nothing I wouldn't do / I just want to be your only one.* Smiling, I longed to launch into a sprint on the track we'd just passed, a burst of exercise fueled by romantic desire. I stayed by his side instead, soaking in songs whose words I hoped were messages he was trying to send me.

"I have a lot to show you," he said. I grasped for the words the moment they left his lips, hoping to claim them before they dissipated like vapor in the air between us. I wanted them in writing, forever inked into my skin. They held too much meaning to just disappear like that. After reaching the school, we embraced by the front doors—I yearned for so much more—but *I have a lot to show you* carried greater weight than a kiss. The sentence repeated in my mind like an incantation I could only pray would come true. I couldn't fathom a reality where it wouldn't.

After that afternoon, I listened to nothing but Blink-182. While Matt rehearsed his plays, I lay in bed staring at my ceiling as *Cheshire Cat* blasted in my earphones. Closing my eyes, I relived our short sunlit walk while the rowdy guitars and sloppy vocals somehow transported me into a state of tranquility. I wanted Matt to show me more bands, to star in more plays I could help him practice lines for. Hidden inside our moments together was a quiet promise of forever. Never before had I wanted to get married, yet I found myself immersed in a fantasy of our joint life in a two-story home with a white picket fence and rose bushes. In my mind, he sat reading the newspaper and sipping coffee at the kitchen table as I made breakfast on the stove. I became so lost in these daydreams they nearly manifested as memories.

"Do you like Blink-182?" was the first thing I asked Otto the next time I saw him. He picked me up after I'd taken a shower, climbed out my window, and strolled the vacant streets. I didn't know why he answered my call—I honestly didn't think he would—yet there I was, in his passenger seat again, speeding into the dark.

"No," he proudly scoffed. "Never liked any of that obnoxious punk bullshit. Those dudes don't have anything to say. If they did, they'd be folk musicians."

My face burned with shame. I felt like a kid in

trouble, but I loved how he indirectly disparaged Matt by revealing him as a fraud. "Here," he said, "hold the wheel." I gripped the leather as he opened the glove compartment and grabbed a cassette. He slipped it from its shell and into the slot, pressing play before returning his hand to the wheel as mine retreated. He only ever steered with his left hand, the right one holding his leg or a cigarette. I thought of taking him by the wrist and putting his hand on my thigh.

The delicate voice flowing from the speakers paired perfectly with the soft strum of an acoustic guitar. It felt strange hearing a man's perspective on a relationship as he talked about a woman: *Does she actually think I'm to blame? / Does she really believe that some word of mine could relieve all her pain?* I'd never considered the man's side of a breakup, always assuming they were fine and incapable of heartbreak.

Otto silently swerved in and out of turns as the man sang about waiting around to die. The song was so soaked in despair it felt like Otto's eyes would overflow any second. He always kept them from me, his gaze in a permanent hiding place—I was lucky to get glimpses. I picked up the case that held the tape. Its cover depicted a man at a desk with his eyes closed. I pretended it was Otto when he was younger. I wanted to ask when he last cried, but I didn't.

Even without alcohol, I still felt drunk. Drunk on the melodies, the exasperated voice. Drunk on Otto next to me, no matter how far away he tried to be. Suddenly, he swerved into an empty lot. A body of water stretched eternally before us, the horizon and waves blending into a single dark wall. He put the car in park, rolled down a window, and lit a cigarette, the music still floating around and between us. Fear crept in as I realized I was alone with a man old enough to be my father. For a moment, I imagined him waving a gun and having his way with me before pulling the trigger. It would be poetic to lose my virginity moments before dying instantly, I thought, or at least a metaphor about what it means to be a girl or something. I brushed off the idea, but the image of Otto brandishing a revolver remained glowing in my head like a religious icon.

"My wife hates him," he said, rupturing my daze. My heart sank at the sound of a word I never expected to hear, a word I forgot existed until now. "I think it's 'cause she hears her sadness in his. Whenever I put this tape on, she turns it off right after the first note. She says he was a drunk, a junkie, a fiend. As if she isn't. As if we all aren't."

"You think we all are?"

"Absolutely," he said. "I had a brother who worked at a repair shop all day before slipping into a tanning bed and laying there 'til his skin turned bronze. It went on like that for years. He lied to me, lied to his wife—he'd lie to anyone if it got him another few hours under those lamps in that hot coffin of his. It wasn't long 'til he got skin cancer and died. Everybody's got some vice. Some just kill you quicker than others."

I thought of Matt's desperate desire to please his parents and astound an audience—his addiction to validation. It must have scared him when I overwhelmed him with affection. All he wanted was to be seen—and I saw him. What worse could happen to a person? I thought of the rush liquor delivered with every swig, how the bottle imbued me with a sensation I wanted to feel all the time. Why else were we put on Earth except to be consumed by what compels us?

Rain fell as if on cue, dripping rhythms on a windshield blurring into an impromptu movie screen. Otto tossed his cigarette, shut the windows, and turned the wipers on, slicing the scene to pieces. Lightning electrified the sky, vivid purple strings I wanted to wear as a necklace. I concealed my fear when the thunder boomed and the hurricane hit. My brother and I used to build forts out of furniture, blankets, and pillows, makeshift shelters doubling as new spaces to explore. I never minded rain or lightning—both mesmerized me—but the violence of thunder convinced me the world was ending, the sound of the universe being torn at the seams.

"I didn't know you had a wife," I said.

"You remind me of her," he replied. "Well, not *you* specifically. Just the way you were throwing up the other night."

Seeing my confusion, he clarified, "When I first met my wife, she was outside a bar throwing up just like you. I held her hair back for her, and that's how we started talking."

"Romantic," I said.

"I thought so, too," he chuckled. "I liked the idea of meeting someone in this vulnerable, disgusting state. It made me feel like I really knew her," he said. "But then we'd go to bars, and she'd always end up throwing up—even if she wasn't drinking that much. Everyone went up to her and asked if she was alright. I got to being less and less sympathetic. Then I realized she was sticking her fingers down her throat—doing it on purpose, wanting people to feel bad for her, to make sure she was OK."

We sat in silence with no track of time, the downpour sending endless ripples through the waves. I had no clue what to say, but that's what

I liked about Otto—he never made me feel like I had to know. "You get to a certain age when you realize everybody's been playing pretend all along," he said, "while you've just been yourself. Foolishly, stupidly…yourself."

Foolishly and stupidly, I leaned in to kiss him. He was startled at first, but then his lips made way for mine, all saliva and smoke so foreign the fear suddenly returned. I felt myself shrink into something small and scared and exposed. Relief rushed through me when a siren shattered the moment like a mirror. I opened my eyes to the sight of red and blue lights. A man in uniform emerged from the car parked behind ours. He tapped Otto's window, making both of us flinch. Chaos was unspooling so fast, and neither of us had time to react. "Hello, officer," Otto said, his voice deeper than normal. A switch flipped—a new Otto emerged.

"*Licenseandregistration*," the officer regurgitated: flashback to the time my mom got pulled over for swerving the car with me and my brother on board.

Luckily, her blood alcohol level was just under the limit. The whole way home, she shouted how it was all our fault, that we'd been distracting her while she drove.

Otto reached into the center console, rummaging through crushed water bottles and crumpled Camel packs to find a small piece of paper. Removing his wallet from his back pocket, he retrieved his license and handed it with the paper through the window. The officer snatched both and trudged back to the safety of the squad car.

I wondered if we kissed or if I just imagined it. My leg trembled as I searched the sky for answers. I yearned to crawl inside a constellation like a ceiling panel and come back out after all this was over. Otto stubbornly kept his spontaneous vow of silence, but I saw his leg shaking, too—our nerves synchronized. He brought his fingers to his mouth and nibbled at the nails, shrinking the nubs even closer to nothing. After tapping the dash became too distracting, he reached for the radio nob to lower the music—which I hadn't realized was still playing—until it was so low the man's voice was nearly nonexistent.

The officer returned to tell us the beach was closed and we were trespassing. When he asked us what we were doing out there in the middle of a storm, Otto played the role of my uncle again, said he had been teaching me to drive. Talking turned into arguing, and I clinged to the man's discreet singing, seeking hope in his voice but finding only doom.

"I need both of you to exit the vehicle," the officer demanded.

Otto and I got drenched as soon as we stepped out of the car. Wiping our faces with wetter hands, we bowed our heads but had nowhere to hide. The officer—soaked but uncaring—told us to stand up straight with our arms out wide. He ran his hands over Otto's sopping clothes, patting extra times on top of his pockets. Then he did the same to me, pausing when his fingers reached my bomber. I froze. "What's in here?" he asked. I couldn't answer. He reached in and pulled out the bag. The bag Dave had slid so secretively into my hand, the bag so small I'd completely forgotten about it. I thought I'd been blessed, but I suddenly felt cursed. It was like he planted it on me, planning my disaster. Maybe Leo was right when he warned me. Maybe Dave really was a demon.

"I—I—" I stuttered mindlessly.

"She's not really my niece," Otto admitted. "I was just dealing drugs to her. That's why we're here."

"How old are you?" the officer asked me.

"Eighteen," I lied. My seventeenth birthday was just a couple months away, the truth close enough to count. What did we have to lose anyway?

I couldn't make out much beyond the whirlwind of mayhem: red and blue lights flashed against the uproarious bay as lightning transformed the sky into a shattered screen, the rain rendering everything a kaleidoscopic version of itself. Nothing was real—only the flood and the noise, the sirens, the thunder, the cop and Otto shouting back and forth, words I heard but failed to understand.

The officer looked at Otto and shook his head in disgust. Through the ruckus, I heard Otto grunt after the officer shoved him up against the hood of his car. I released a shriek, incapable of offering anything coherent. There were three cop cars now—I hadn't even noticed when the others arrived. The officer ushered Otto into one of them and out of my sight.

Another officer approached and led me to his vehicle. I felt more danger in the shelter of the cop car than outside in the storm. Processing what had happened—that Otto was arrested and it was all my fault—I burst into tears. When we left the parking lot, I watched Otto's lonely car disappear into the distance and wondered what would happen to it. I imagined the man still singing about death as the waves surged and swallowed his song.

4.
Impossible Bliss

In the bath again, lips locked on my knee, teeth digging in. Skin shriveled from so many nights in hot water.

The cop took me home to report my misbehavior to my mom. As the sky unleashed its fury on the streets, she invited him inside. "Go to your room while we talk," she shouted, and I obeyed. Pressing my ear to the door, I heard her reveal my true age. This new information seemed to evoke some sympathy from the officer, who said I could be excluded from the investigation since I was a minor. "Who's this man you mentioned?" I heard my mother ask. I knew she'd ask me soon, too. *Who's this man?* I wondered. I honestly had no clue. All I knew was he wasn't the bad guy they made him out to be.

My mom grounded me and installed an alarm system that monitored all the doors and windows, emitting a telltale screech when any opened. I didn't bother fighting it. Instead, I tried answering her questions. "He's just a dealer who hangs around the high school," I attempted. "I was getting it for Vivian," I added unconvincingly.

It was cocaine. The lie made me feel like a bad person. Not for being dishonest with my mom—that was the easy part—but for throwing Otto and Vivian under the bus. I didn't think Otto would want me to tell the truth, that he was a man I just liked talking to and being around. "You should never be in a car with a forty-one-year-old man," my mom scolded, the number floating through my mind. He was twice my age, plus nine.

With little else to do, I began plotting Otto's escape—but without his last name, it would be impossible to find any information about his arrest online. When I pressed my mom, she divulged that Otto was in jail and no one had paid his bond. I daydreamt about entering the nearest bank with a gun and demanding obscene amounts of cash. I suddenly understood why people did bad things. It didn't seem like a bad thing to me, though—stealing money for a good purpose. Was this why my father left? Did he think it would be for the better? I shouldn't assume, I thought. Trying to guess people's intentions is a fool's errand.

Maybe I didn't need to rob a bank. Maybe the answer was right in front of me: the Internet—a place where people were always giving money away. All I needed were the right words, the best lies. *My poor grandmother just got diagnosed with dementia, and we need money to pay her caretakers. My baby cousin has cancer, and I'm raising money for his medical bills.* Maybe the answer awaited in "Waiting Around To Die"—I bring the little cash I have to a casino and gamble until I get the thousands I need. For a moment the world unfurled before me, everything easy and plausible.

Invigorated by the idea, I took the first online survey I found. It promised me twenty bucks, but I fell asleep halfway through, my laptop falling from my bed to the floor before I could cash in. It took everything in me not to scream at the top of my lungs when I discovered its shattered screen the next morning.

I started going stir-crazy after that little mishap. It was April, and I missed the parties. The flash of teenage recklessness of which I finally got a liquor-laden taste only made me yearn for more. Now that I'd felt the buzz, I could never go back to who I was: the girl who preferred staying home and lying in bed, wasting away in the bath, reading books sprawled out across the floor. The more I stayed inside, the more my memories of Otto faded and my heartbreak over Matt sharpened. I pictured them on opposite ends of a seesaw, my feelings a gust of wind shifting the upper hand on a whim. I imagined Otto lifting Matt up in the air with one hand and punching him down to the ground with the other. Otto was the one in trouble, but I needed him to be my savior.

My grades fell, but I was too focused on real problems to notice. After meeting Otto, I realized everything inside those drab tan walls was fake. None of it mattered—it was just a bubble that popped the moment you went outside. I suddenly understood Dave's antics, his tantrums against teachers and the other students. Why respect total strangers telling us what to do? I skipped most of my classes, but when I did attend, I ended up slumped over my desk in a languished haze, drained of life from staying up all night thinking about Otto—if only to avoid thinking about Matt. I no longer knew which was worse. My geometry teacher sent me to the principal's office after hearing the soft static of music buzzing from my earbuds while she filled the chalkboard with formulas foreign to me as another language. Polly taught me her method: hide the phone in your hoodie, slide the wires through its sleeves, and rest your head on your hand, covering the earbud. I wondered how much trouble I'd get in for smuggling songs into class. Ms. Mason had it out for me ever since my scores dropped below the seventies. She erupted into shouting fits each time she spotted the string sticking out from my hoodie's cuff, but I couldn't hear a thing she said as Townes' tranquil melancholy permeated my skull. Anger aged her face, casting a cartoonish rage from eyes burning into but never through me.

One night, I heard Simon's Mustang rumbling outside. Peeking through my blinds, I saw Vivian hanging out the passenger window as her waving hand beckoned. Desperate to escape, I tiptoed to the alarm system and disabled it. Even the beep of each button couldn't keep my mom from snoring. I quickly slid on my slip and went out the window—a maneuver I'd dearly missed.

I never told Vivian what happened with Otto, but she hadn't informed me of her reconciliation with Simon, either. It was like our friendship only existed in the throes of exhilaration. I was on my own otherwise, but I didn't mind. It seemed it was just who I was and how I was meant to live.

"Where are we going?" I asked.

Vivian replied by handing me a mini of whiskey. I nearly gagged as I downed it—whiskey was hard for me to enjoy, the flavor too sweet. I preferred liquor that tasted like death, not candy. "Dave's," Vivian said casually, like I should know. After seeing me finish the mini, she handed me another—this time vodka—and it went down like water.

Lampposts speckled the black night with orange streaks as I pressed my cheek to the window. The passing homes rested with no lights on, safe in their sleep. I longed to be nocturnal, to live forever in this dim emptiness. I wanted to climb into their lives through their windows the way I returned to mine each dawn. Above all, I wanted to be their daughter, their sister, their mother—anything.

"That little bitch better not fuckin' be there,"

said Simon.

"You mean Leo?" Vivian asked. "Don't make a scene. He was just playing the game."

Simon slammed the brakes and the car suddenly stopped. My face hit against the soft back of his seat as Vivian's head narrowly dodged the dashboard. "What the fuck," she spat.

"Don't you fucking talk to me like that," he said, his gaze still straight ahead.

I hated Simon. From the backseat, he was nothing but a faceless force of anger. I never knew why Vivian was with him, but I didn't know why I put up with his shit, either. Maybe it was just our mutual inability to say no, our tendency to get in any car with a stranger offering us a ride.

Teens ran in circles on the lawn as '80s tunes boomed out through the open screen door. Simon circled the block and parked in the same spot as before. Inside, every room reeked of weed and people did shots to "Head Over Heels." Dave scolded every stoner he spotted, telling them where to shove their joints when he wasn't yelling for someone to turn down the music. He smiled when he saw me, but I didn't know why.

"Did you enjoy my present?" he asked. "I only give to people I *really* care about."

I couldn't tell him the truth or punch him in the face like I'd wanted to. It wasn't his fault, anyway. Instead, I said, "What's my name?"

He paused and scratched the top of his head. "Amanda?"

"Strike one."

"Fuck," he said. "There's strikes? Well, gimme a minute. It's on the tip of my tongue, though."

I was flattered by his flirting attempts, allowing myself the pleasure of feeling desired, one I wasn't offered very often. Dave was no Otto—nor was he Matt—but he was dangerous, and that was enough. Vivian already disappeared, a magic trick I'd gotten used to. I needed someone to latch onto, and who better than the host?

Dave flitted to the kitchen and I followed. He

sighed after seeing a beer spill on the floor. "I gotta figure out how to get this music turned down," he said.

"I'll clean up," I said. I liked cleaning—washing dishes right after eating, vacuuming dust bunnies under the bed, mopping to procrastinate homework.

He thanked me and ran off. On my knees, I absorbed the puddle with paper towels and sprayed Windex, wiping until the stench went away. Brown work boots walked in, already staining the green tiles with dirt. "Cinderella?" a voice said. I looked up—it was Leo.

I stood up. "Not smart to be here," I said, looking over his shoulder for Simon, fearing what lay ahead.

"Not smart for any of us to be here."

He wasn't wrong.

"You know, it's weird," he continued. "You didn't even know who Dave was, then I told you all that bad stuff about him. Now you're talking to him."

"It's weird," I said. "You didn't know who Vivian was and then you were kissing her."

"Come on. That was a game."

"So is this," I said, though I didn't really know what I meant.

The Cure's "Just Like Heaven" came on, and finally the volume was regulated, no longer booming. I pushed past Leo and poured myself gin. As I sipped, I noticed Dave on the back porch beckoning me to come out. I slid the screen door, and it fell off its hinges. "Don't worry about that," he said charmingly.

Dave was sitting with two girls who introduced themselves as Shelby and Ginny. They were all smoking cigarettes, and suddenly my fingers felt awkward, clumsy without anything between them. As if he could hear my thoughts, Dave held one out. "Want one?"

I accepted. He held out a flame for me. The tobacco tasted almost chocolatey. "It's so fucked up," Shelby said to Ginny, shaking her head.

"What is?" I asked.

Shelby sighed, expressing a disinterest in repeating whatever story she'd just shared. "Her grandmother was scammed," Ginny explained. "Someone called and said Shelby got into a bad car accident, and they needed $40,000 from her for hospital bills or else they couldn't treat her. She didn't know how to wire money, so she took the cash out of the bank, put it in a shoebox, and put it in the backseat of a black car. That's what they instructed her to do. It's so crazy that people get away with this. What could they possibly need money that bad for?"

I hid my smile. Suddenly, it felt like the night was a revelation. I didn't believe in God, but it felt like some higher power put Shelby and Ginny in front of me just so I could hear this—my answer to freeing Otto. "That's terrible," I said, exhaling smoke. My secret sat in my chest obediently like a bird perched inside a cage.

"Luckily, my parents can't even pick up any

phone calls," Dave quipped. Shelby and Ginny exploded with laughter and apologies, feeling guilty for finding humor in something dark, as if he hadn't been the one to say it. I forced a giggle.

Shelby and Ginny went inside to do shots. Dave and I were alone. "What's your favorite song?" he asked.

I worried there was a right or wrong answer, but I didn't know enough about him to know what he liked or didn't like. "I've been listening to 'Waiting Around To Die' by Townes Van Zandt a lot," I said, nervous.

His eyes widened. "Damn," he said. "What's wrong?"

I chuckled and looked down at my diminishing cigarette.

"That's my bad," he continued. "I shouldn't have given you an upper. You're a downers girl." He reached into his pocket and pulled out a thin white pill that resembled a Tic Tac. "Take this," he said, placing it in my palm.

"What is it?" I asked, twirling it between my fingers, examining it though there was nothing to see except blankness.

"Xanax," he said.

I thought about saying something about my brother in rehab in the desert, the grip that alcohol and tiny capsules had on him, but instead I said nothing. I gave it back to him. "You don't want it?" he asked.

"Put it on my tongue," I said.

With his thumb and forefinger, he dropped the drug onto my tastebuds, and I swallowed. He looked calm, sweet; I wanted to ask if what I'd heard about him was true, but I didn't want to ruin the moment. He started talking about a musician named Elliott Smith, but I couldn't hear his words because I was distracted by the softness spreading through my body, the weightlessness that made me feel as if I could fly. He laughed as my eyelids drooped and a lazy smile spread across my face. He took my hands in his and shook me but I was drifting, unbothered. Then he was looking at his phone, his face lit white by the screen. He procured headphones and put them over my ears. I was transported to an even more peaceful world, surrounded by serenity, an acoustic guitar like a cloud I was floating on. The delicate singing came from a voice I'd simultaneously never heard before and known my whole life. This impossible bliss stretched out forever, I was running through the desert, I was jumping off a rooftop, I was soaring through a city skyline.

From the corner of my eye, Dave, who appeared more as a shadow than a human, shot out of his seat and disappeared inside. I slowly removed the headphones. In the distance, I heard screams, glass shattering, bodies against walls, bodies against floors, more shattering, more screams, but it was all so far away, like a thunderstorm in the sky of another planet. In my slivered vision, two shadows wrestled, their shadow arms on each other's throats, shoulders, faces; another shadow became entangled, trying to pull them apart. For a second, fear crept in on me, disturbed by this grotesque dance, but the wave of fatigue settled over me like a blanket, and I was safe.

I woke to Vivian shaking me. "Come *on*," she grunted, eventually mustering the strength to pull me up on my feet. "We have to get out of here. I'm going to call Otto."

We staggered down the porch steps onto the dewy grass, then around the house to the front. "You can't," I slurred. "He's in jail."

"*What?*"

"It's a long story," I said. "But I'm going to get him out, so it's all OK."

She stomped her black heel into the ground and threw her hands to the sky. "How the hell are we going to get home?"

Despite my all-consuming haze, I dragged one foot in front of the other, one foot in front of the other, and the pattern became a comfort. I didn't want to stop. On the crumbling sidewalks of residential neighborhoods, Vivian and I walked and walked and walked, sometimes collapsing on the grass and having the other pull us back up, sometimes stumbling but always catching our balance.

"This is poetic," I blurted.

"Pathetic?"

"*Poetic.*"

The air was warm with a gentle breeze, and the stars glowed promisingly. I told Vivian that I hated Simon, and she said she did, too. I wondered if, underneath Dave's charm and sensitivity, he held the same rage as Simon, the same urge to throw fists, to hit the brakes until a head hits a hard surface, to knock glass onto the floor, to find pleasure in cruelty. Then I wondered the same about Otto. Dawn was breaking as we embraced each other underneath a flickering streetlamp before splitting to enter our separate neighborhoods.

5.
You Loved Me Then And You Do Now

A couple hours after finally falling into bed, I woke up disoriented, my mom shouting in my face, yelling that the alarm system was disabled and I must have snuck out last night and I didn't care about anyone's safety. As my eyelids slowly fluttered open and my life seeped back into me, I was offended, yelling back that she had some nerve to accuse me of such a thing, that she probably forgot to activate it yesterday before bed, that I'd done nothing but sleep and she better leave me alone. With that, she went quiet and exited my room, closing the door behind her.

My legs were sore from the walk home. I didn't remember falling, but my knee was scraped, a bright red circle like a supergiant sun, so different from the faint purple blobs that typically adorned my legs. What stuck out to me most from the previous evening was the epiphany I'd had. A phone call that led to tens of thousands of dollars. When my mom left for work, I flipped through the yellow phonebook. It was pretty easy to spot the elderly—names like Gertrude, Betty, and Agatha gave away the old ladies.

Using star sixty-seven, I began calling. I knew the chance of the women picking up was scarce, and the chance of them believing me was even lower. Therefore, I had to start as soon as possible. I inked bubbles around the old-timey names and crossed them out as I traveled down the list. Some exclaimed that they didn't even have a daughter; others erupted with curses: "You really think I'd fall for this bullshit?" I simultaneously applauded and resented them. After an hour of bad luck, an old lady with a quivering voice responded with sincere worry.

"What do I need to do?" she asked, her voice rising with each word.

"You need to go to the bank, take out $40,000, tell me your address, and I will pull up to your house, you will put the money in the backseat, and we will rush it to the hospital and treat your daughter for her injuries. But you have to stay on the line with me as you do this."

"Oh, dear," she lamented. "Let me find my keys."

I couldn't believe my luck, but I had to hold any sense of hope at arm's length. I knew there were many opportunities for it all to go wrong, that it was fragile, hanging on by a loose thread. I put her on speaker and texted Vivian that I needed a ride from Simon as soon as possible. I added that I would pay him two hundred dollars. Soon enough, as Edith was en route to her bank to get the money, Simon's blue Mustang buzzed outside my house. I hopped in the passenger seat. Edith told me her address. It was twenty minutes away.

Simon went ninety on the highway. When I asked if he could slow down, he hit the gas harder. I worried we would get pulled over and my plan would be ruined. But there was nothing I could do. I turned to Simon and saw nothing behind his eyes. A bruise turned his jaw purple, I assumed from a blow from Leo. On my walk home with Vivian, she informed me that Simon came up behind Leo and pushed him onto the floor. After that, mayhem—the two ghosts I had been watching in slow motion, then Dave intervening.

Edith lived in a nice neighborhood of Tudor houses with lawns decorated with bushes and flowers sprawled out over dirt. Her home was an inviting yellow. "Now what?" Simon asked. Edith said she was almost home. We waited until her beige 2008 Toyota Camry rolled down the road at twenty miles an hour, then sluggishly pulled into her driveway. Simon whispered under his breath, "What the fuck?"

From her trunk, Edith procured a walker, wheeling herself over to the car. A big brown paper bag poked out of her crimson pocketbook. I instructed Simon to crack the window in the backseat, but not enough for her to see us. Protected by the anonymity of tinted windows, we ducked as Edith dropped the bag onto the backseat, the bills slipping out onto the floor, wrapped up in currency straps. She pleaded for us to take care of her daughter and thanked us before Simon sped away, going through the stop sign and turning so hard that my whole body hit the door. Simon was sputtering swear words interspersed with laughs of disbelief; when I tried to interrupt him to explain, he only repeated, "What the fuck? What the fuck?" with a giant smile on his face.

He pulled up in front of my house and unlocked the doors. I got out, leaving the passenger door open as I walked over to the backseat to retrieve the money. Before I could reach for the handle, Simon hit the gas, nearly running over my foot, the passenger door almost hitting a tree, still ajar, until down the block he slammed on the brakes and it shut. I stood with my mouth open, no thoughts in my head, just an anger toward him that I imagined similar to the anger that always filled him, the kind of anger that prompts him to shatter glass and take a fist to someone's face. But the anger was directed toward myself for trusting him. I reasoned that I didn't have a choice, nor did I have time to think anything through. In that moment, still upright on the sidewalk, I yearned to swan dive onto the pavement of the road, to welcome the collision against the asphalt to make me bleed, and then allow cars passing by to tear the viscera out of me. Instead, I shook my whole body the way a dog does. I shook off the suicidal ideation and let out a massive scream into the bright blue sky as if I could rupture it, as if I could communicate to the world that something bad just happened to me. It was a glitch in the universe. It needed to be undone.

The shriek did nothing. I walked back inside my house and flopped onto my bed like nothing had happened. I remembered Dave's mention of Elliott Smith the night prior. I took out my phone and put my earbuds in and pressed play on his self-titled album. I stared at the ceiling and wanted to cry almost instantly. His voice was quiet yet searing. I felt as if he was lying next to me, telling me about his pain as well as mine, like it had become one. I felt mutilated by my want, disfigured and evil. But when I thought of goodness, I no longer knew what it was. I wondered if I'd ever truly known it. I thought maybe it was the first thing I knew, but as I knew more things, I knew goodness less and less. I heard the resentment seething in the songs and pulsating in my ears, captivated by how it could sound so beautiful and delicate. *No bad dream fucker's gonna boss me around.* I felt he understood me in a way I could not yet understand myself.

As he sang about walking around with an open container from 7-Eleven, the music paused, and my phone vibrated. *Unknown caller.* I answered. An automated voice said the call was from a prison. I shot up so fast I almost fell. I pressed 1 to accept the call, as instructed, then waited, kicking my feet, for Otto's voice to emerge. When it did, he sounded tired, irritated, even just within one word: "Hello?" The *hell* prominent, the *o* barely hanging on.

Nervously, I said, "Hi."

I didn't know what to say. I wanted to ask how he was able to call me, if he had memorized my phone number before getting locked up, but he answered my questions before I could muster the courage to ask: "Luckily, I got a glance at my phone before they put me away. Sang the numbers in my head like a song. Probably know it better than you at this point."

I smiled. "I'm getting you out," I blurted. He laughed, then it turned into a sigh. I continued, "I'm serious."

His line went silent. "Please tell me you haven't done anything." Irritation filtered into his tone again. I was quiet. "Listen to me, OK?" he said. "Don't worry about me. I don't want to get out. The truth is I belong here. OK? You might not think so, but you don't know me or what I've done. So you have to stay out of this and let it happen. Do you hear me?"

I tried to swallow, but my throat was dry. I tried to speak, but only a cough came out. Finally, I said, "What do you mean?"

"I mean, there are things you don't know about me. I should be in here," he said. "Goddammit, why are you even asking questions? This has nothing to do with you. You just have to accept it. Can you do that? You know what, I'm not even going to ask that. You have to do that. You don't have a choice."

Tears welled up in my eyes. I only wanted to say things I knew were stupid. *What about our kiss? I thought I would get to know you? How are you going to pick me up when I call you saying I need a ride? Am I still your Baby Bruise?* "I'm sorry," I said.

"Don't be," he said. "You didn't do anything wrong."

I realized he didn't know anything about me

either.

We said goodbye and hung up. Elliott's voice resumed singing. *Oh, we're so very precious, you and I / And everything that you do makes me want to die.* Everything I wanted to tell him was bubbling inside of me, begging to be let out. I didn't know what to do with myself, so I sat at my desk, ripped out a piece of lined paper from a notebook, and began writing a letter to Otto. The words flowed from me in a deluge. I felt lighter and lighter as my pen crossed the page, as the pages piled up one over another, as my infatuation was finally taking a tangible form instead of floating around inside me shapelessly. I wrote of how I felt about our moments together, how I felt when I was away from him, how I fantasized about so much more with him, how I imagined, before prison, he sat on his porch smoking cigarettes and reflecting on his life, and I wanted to be there, sitting beside him exhaling smoke, telling him that there was still so much more life to live. I saw it so vividly in my head—it had to be real, and if it wouldn't happen in this life, it certainly occurred in a past one. Because of that call, I finally knew which prison he was in; I looked up the address and wrote it on the back of an envelope.

The sun was about to set. I jolted, ink skidding across the page, at a harsh thud erupting from behind me. I turned and saw Vivian waving at my window. I smirked and rose to let her in. It was still early in the evening, the alarm system not yet activated.

"Put on something cute," she said. "We're going to the school play."

I shuddered. "Why?"

"So we can boo Matt," she said. "Duh."

I didn't want to do that, but I was curious about the performance, considering I'd helped him prepare for the role. I wanted to watch everyone in the audience watching him. I didn't know why. It was a kind of masochism.

Vivian slid my closet open. She picked out a white lace top and a black skirt. Without resistance, I took them from her and put them on. I put on my bomber since a chill remained even though it was almost May. I told my mom we were off to the play, and she permitted it since it was a school event. For once, Vivian and I left out the front door, and we walked the twenty minutes to the school. Before we left my block, she pulled out two minis from her purse. Wordlessly, we slammed one each, then tossed the empty bottles into my neighbor's garbage bin. The buzz hit sweetly, enlivened by the traffic of the main road, the headlights turning on, and the men in their car windows looking us up and down before speeding off.

"What was that favor you had Simon do?" Vivian asked. "He hasn't talked to me since. He's gone radio silent. I don't get it."

"Why do you need to get it? He's an asshole," I said.

"Yeah," she said, "but he gave us free rides."

"We can find someone else, someone less shitty," I said.

We left it at that. As we ambled alongside each

other on the crosswalk, I reached into the pocket of my jacket and felt an object I couldn't identify. My hand wrapped around it and recognized its shape—a pill bottle. Once we reached the other side of the street, I pulled it out and read the label. Xanax.

"Whoa," Vivian said. "Where did you get that?"

I handed it over to her and she examined it. "Dave must've given it to me."

She laughed in disbelief. "He is known for this sort of thing," she said. "He's been prescribed a lot of stuff over the years. He never took it, only stashed it up. Then gives them away like party favors."

I frowned at the comparison, like he gave them away to just anyone, not only me. I didn't know why I cared. She unscrewed the cap and popped one into her mouth, uncaring of the vehicles surrounding us. She gave the bottle back to me, and I did the same before putting it back in my pocket. I wondered where Simon was, if he had anything keeping him here. He could've been halfway across the country in his obnoxious car, mistaking $40,000 for $400,000, starting a new life. Did Edith find out it was all a scam yet? Did she cry? I brushed off these spiraling thoughts. Vivian and I trudged up the hill leading to the school, the cars of seniors and parents passing us.

Throngs of people stood out front, being let in. We joined the crowd and waited until we were finally within reach of the door. I felt that familiar softness humming through me. "Ticket?" the student at the door said.

"We don't have," Vivian muttered. "Can we buy two?"

"Sorry," he said, "sold out."

Vivian and I looked each other and stepped away. A glimmer in her eye informed me she had a plan. She took my hand and guided me along the perimeter of the school. It looked so different at night, so much more alluring. I could tell Vivian was as excited to break us into the building as I had been to break Otto out of prison.

The sidewalk was cracked, the sky darkening into a deep blue. We reached the back of the school, Vivian walking a few steps ahead of me. She waved me over to a window left ajar. "Mr. Williams is an idiot," she said. "He always has the window open." We climbed into the classroom, which was dark and musty, our feet landing on the beige tiles. The chalkboard was not erased, barely legible notes about *Jane Eyre* still strewn about for an invisible audience to read. The setup of desks looked filled with ghosts.

"Come on," Vivian said, already halfway to the door, while I was lost in the ethereal emptiness of the space.

I followed her, and we scampered down the hall, trying to suppress our mischievous giggles. We rounded the corner and headed toward the door of the auditorium. The play was about to start. We noticed a couple of vacant seats in the back and quickly plopped into them before anyone could realize we didn't belong there.

Vivian procured, again, two minis from her

purse, as if it contained an entire supply. I gave her a perplexed look, and she sent me a gaze that said *Don't question it*. She was a hedonist magician. We ducked and let the liquid slide down our throats; I was pleasantly surprised as I realized it was tequila, imbued with the joy that it always brought.

The lights went out, a blackness taking over everything. The curtains were drawn, and classmates I'd never interacted with paced back and forth on the stage, wearing modest black dresses that reached the floor and white bonnets on their heads. A spotlight formed a white glowing circle they walked in and out of. They were shrieking and shouting and emitting all sorts of disturbing noises that made me cover my ears with my hands. The ritual ended with the girls screaming and running away, though my vision was too hazy to see what had happened. My leg bounced up and down impatiently.

A bed was rolled out, and more lights turned on. Two people argued as a woman lay in bed. My eyes continued to lose focus, a dizziness unfurling, restlessness spreading through me at a rapid rate. That was when Matt entered the stage, his baritone forced to its lowest possible level. I sunk into the red cushion of my seat, watching as Polly played the role of Abigail, taking Matt's hand in hers for a second before he retracted his fingers, rejecting her with an obviousness he couldn't even offer me. Did that make it better or worse? Did he care about me enough to not want to hurt my feelings with a clear rejection, or did he not care about me at all and just found it easier to avoid me? I didn't like being avoided, ignored.

Polly looked so pathetic as Abigail, trying to convince Matt to love her. *I know how you clutched my back behind your house and sweated like a stallion whenever I come near! I saw your face when she put me out, and you loved me then, and you do now!* Before I could process what was happening, my body shot out of its seat and left the theater, a reaction as instinctual as puking up rotten food. I opened my eyes, and I was outside the school on the grass, my back against the wall, my face stained with tears. Quickly, Vivian appeared.

"That's not me," my mouth said. Disembodied, I wasn't in control of anything I was doing. Different parts of me kept doing things without my permission. But I knew what those words meant— Polly, Abigail, was not me. I was not a girl who pleaded for someone to requite her love. I couldn't be. Not with Matt, not with Otto. But I was—I wanted to bruise my knees kneeling at their feet.

Vivian nodded like she knew what I was saying and pulled me up. We moved so slowly that the twenty-minute walk home took us double the time. I cried quietly because I couldn't stop. In my head, Elliott Smith sang to me. *The things that you tell yourself / They'll kill you in time.*

6.
Captive

In bed, I felt as if I were lying in the wreckage of the past couple of months. I held the pill bottle Dave gave me like it was a totem, a token of his love, of anyone's love, because that's all I wanted, after all. I wanted to give myself to anyone who was willing to take me, if such a person existed. I didn't know how this happened, when desperation took me by the throat. The more rejections I was faced with, the more I needed the warmth of someone else. I felt terribly naïve, especially since no one had ever entered my body. I was about to turn seventeen.

Dave was throwing a party the night before my seventeenth birthday. While my mom slept, I initiated my routine of disabling the alarm and climbing out the window. After a few minutes, a maroon Honda Civic rolled up, a man named Kevin behind the wheel. According to Vivian, he was a friend of Dave's. He greeted me as I crawled into the backseat, a nicety that Simon never even bothered to offer. Vivian flashed a big smile at me—teeth and everything—holding out a tequila bottle that was about the size of my hand. "For your birthday," she said.

I sipped the liquor on the ride, which was a nice change of pace as Kevin exceeded the speed limit at only five or ten miles rather than double. When he used the brakes, his foot settled on it gradually instead of slamming on the pedal.

The party was more crowded than the others, people spilling out of the front and back doors, cigarette smoke clouding the kitchen and alcohol already on low supply. I tried not to look for Dave, but my eyes wandered, in search of his disheveled brown hair or his syrupy eyes. I reached into my pocket and popped a Xanax as if it would provide me the answer, bring me closer to him.

My materiality fizzled out and I became nothing but a cardboard cutout amongst alive people whose arms dangled over each other and whose mouths talked while sharing cigarettes and sipping each other's drinks. Miles away, Otto sat in prison uninterested in leaving, yet no matter where I was, I had the urge to exit, to run away. But where would I go? I wanted nonexistence, or maybe I just wanted to return to who I was before my first heartbreak. I couldn't reverse time, but I could drink until I reached the place of wonderful nothingness. I stumbled to the back porch, pushing past bodies, taking swigs of my tequila, and bumming a cigarette off of anyone who would let me. I felt like being sloppy, like being rude. In an hour or so, I would turn seventeen. I had the right to be a bitch. I was constantly plunging deeper into a bottomless malaise. As two guys talked about walking to the gas station to pick up more beer, I bragged about having my own source of alcohol, waving my half-drunk liquor bottle like a trophy, slurring about how prepared I was, even though Vivian had surprised me with it.

The lingerers on the back porch ignored my declaration and acted as if I was invisible when I walked over to the side of the house and threw up in the grass. My hair fell around my face like curtains because no one was there to hold it back. I stayed paralyzed, staring into the puddle I'd painted on the ground as if it were a portal I could jump into to teleport anywhere else. But where? I reached into my pocket, swallowed another pill.

I couldn't find Vivian anywhere. Back inside, I picked up a Solo cup with indecipherable clear liquid and chugged it. To my relief, it was poison. My tequila was a third of the way gone, and I was growing worried. When I turned around, I bumped into Kevin. I slurred that I thought he was with Vivian. He said he didn't know where she was either; he hadn't seen her in a while. He followed me as I shoved through the throng and down the narrow corridor, pulling at every knob in sight, doors opening like curtains falling. I anxiously anticipated the big reveal of what Vivian was really up to.

It was the final door on the right. I swung it so hard it hit the wall. Vivian's shirt was off, her back to me, her legs wrapped around Dave, whose face crumbled like he'd seen a ghost. He may as well have. Vivian's head turned, and her eyes met mine with horror. She pulled at the white blanket and covered herself, reaching for her clothes and putting them on underneath the sheet.

I walked into the room. "What the fuck?" I spit.

Dave slid his pants on. "What?" he spit back.

I looked to Vivian for help, for understanding, even though she was the one who had wronged me. She stood up and looked me in the eyes without apology. She shouted, "We were just having fun!"

"I'm not having any fun!"

"I fucking know," she yelled. "You never are. You can never have a good fucking time. You can never just have a crush on someone, you have to be *in love* with them. It's not cute to be in love with everyone. It's pathetic."

I looked to Dave, as if he would help me. "You think you're the only person who's miserable," he said. "We all are. But we deal with it instead of making it other people's problems."

"I'm a good friend," Vivian said. "I bring you to these parties, I give you drinks, I help you up when you're on the ground crying. Yet you're never fucking happy. Ever. You're heartbroken over a guy you never even *kissed*."

It was as if she punched me, the way she used my pain over Matt against me. "And I never asked you what happened with Otto," she continued. "Because I don't even want to know what you got yourself into. And I don't know what you did to Simon, either."

We were quiet for a few seconds. When she realized I wouldn't respond, she looked at her phone. "Oh, look," she said. "It's your birthday. Happy fucking birthday." She pushed her way out of the room. Dave offered a shrug before doing the same. I fell to the hardwood floor and hugged my knees to my chest and sucked on my skin as I cried, my teeth digging deep just for the sake of distraction. I imagined hot water filling the room, comforting me with its warmth before drowning me.

In a haze, I left the room and trudged through the maze of shadows until I reached the front door. With painful certainty, I knew no one cared I was leaving. The sky was smeared with stars, and I wondered how many were already dead yet still glowing in that moment. I began the walk I'd done once before with Vivian, this time on my own, my sneakers treading the cracks in the sidewalk, tears turning the cement into a beige orb. Only one more sip of the tequila remained, and I held onto it for as long as I could, proud of my self-discipline. Passing houses of sleeping families, cars parked in driveways, cars hidden under tarps, a rare window lit up with the orange radiance of just one lamp. I longed to press my hands against the glass, beg to be let in, taken care of.

Instead of making it home, I passed out on a park bench. As spectral light cracked through the sky at dawn, I woke up and continued my walk. My phone was dead. I had no clue what time it was as I finally approached my block, but the chirps of birds rang through the air. I noticed that, instead of closing the window as much as possible like I usually did while sneaking out, I had accidentally left it wide open. I shrugged off the mistake, climbed back in. I wanted more alcohol, if only to put me to bed. The walk had been too sobering, and I didn't want to feel anything, remember anything. I took the final sip of my tequila and tiptoed toward the kitchen to my mom's liquor cabinet, when an amorphous screech ricocheted off the walls from my mom's room, sending a wave of fear through my body. "Mom?" I shouted, following the sound. I turned the light on in her bedroom and found her on the floor with duct tape on her mouth, her hands tied to the radiator.

I ran to help her. I ripped the tape off her mouth and she gasped for air. A string of words left her mouth in incoherent utterances. She thrashed her shaking frame and my fingers trembled as they tried to free her from the zip tie. "Hold on," I said, rushing to my room to get scissors, which successfully cut through the thick material. She shot up and paced back and forth maniacally to regain her sanity.

"What happened?" I asked.

She breathed in and out. "Something about $40,000," she said, and I was immediately lightheaded with shock. "These people—these two men—they got in here—I don't know how. The alarm system was off. Maybe I forgot to turn it on again. But still, I don't know what door they came in through or how. They tied me up and said I'd stolen $40,000 from their mother, and they wanted it back. I said I had no clue what they were talking about and I didn't have that money. They said they traced the phone call to this address. I said I didn't know what phone call they were talking about. They resorted to just taking my whole jewelry box and some cash in my wallet. We have to call the police now."

She opened the closet and reached for the top shelf. "They put my phone here," she explained, taking the device and turning it on.

"Wait," I said, grabbing it from her. "Don't call the cops."

"*Why?*"

"It was me," I said. "I stole the $40,000."

Her eyes widened with a rage I'd only ever witnessed in men. I worried she would push me onto the floor or punch me in the face, but she just whispered, "*What?*"

I burst into tears, overwhelmed and steeped in self-loathing. My body, without my permission again, ran out of the room and to the kitchen, crouched in front of the liquor cabinet. I pulled the first bottle I saw from its pocket and twisted off its cap. Before I could bring it to my lips, there my mom was, behind me, feral, grabbing for the bottle. We became entangled in this grotesque dance. I watched from afar, shouting at myself to stop, to give up, but I couldn't break the barrier. Instead, I stood my ground, folding into myself, cradling the bottle in my arms and pulling away from her, but she latched onto me, refusing to let go. I screamed at the top of my lungs as if my voice had the power to make her vanish.

She gripped the bottle with her hands. I tried to push her off, but she held on tight, and we ended up on the floor, the glass slipping from my grasp and shattering, the sour scent puncturing the air. The orange pill bottle rattled as it fell from my pocket, rolling on the cold checkered tiles. Her attention on the liquor immediately transferred onto the Xanax as she took it in her hand and read the label. We pulled away from each other, defeated, breathing heavy.

"What happened to you?" she asked.

Again, instead of offering an explanation, I sobbed.

Later that day, my mom booked me a flight to Arizona to be admitted into the same rehab my brother had gone to. He had left years before to work in California, finding the program to be successful. I wondered how pathetic my mom felt. Both of her children sent states away to get rid of their addictions. It's not fair for her to ask what happened to me, I thought; what happened to me was that I came from your womb, so why don't you tell me what's wrong with me, what's in my blood, my genes. But she still sipped from glass bottles or aluminum cans every night before bed without vomiting or getting enmeshed in chaos. Maybe it was my dad's fault. Maybe it was why he ran away, knowing he'd created monsters. Who could blame him? Maybe it was for the best, to prevent him from ruining us further.

From the plane, I watched the yellow desert sprawl out for miles and miles and felt refreshed by the change of scenery. Cacti were taller than I expected. The facility was ridiculously grandiose, a large underground pool, always a vivid aqua, mountains looming in the distance. I spent days with my toes in the water, wondering what the point of such luxury was if it couldn't be mixed with a delightfully altered state of consciousness. But as the heat intensified, I felt a sweet natural drunkenness from the sweltering air, from the West Coast itself.

Sometimes we embarked on hikes, our feet digging through the endless sands as we navigated the radiant, dry landscape, our breaths ragged and water bottles crushed in our hands as we took desperate sips. The reward was always a delirious sunset. Nature was a necessary reminder that I didn't matter, that life was bigger than the cramped house parties that reverberated with a sense of promise, that those pleasures were ephemeral and followed by hangovers and disillusionment. The only true beauty was that of the Earth, which would also one day collapse into nothing, a long time after I'd collapsed into nothing first, a skeleton in a box in the ground.

In group, I heard about my acquaintances' rock bottoms. Compared to them, my struggles seemed mundane. However, I floored enough former delinquents with my $40,000 story, confessing that I was not just addicted to substances but souls, obsessively searching for intimate connection because it gave me the same high as alcohol or pills did. My bad habits, I learned, were an attempt to fill the void. I remembered what Otto said about his brother being addicted to tanning, about how we're all addicts, we all cope in our own ways, some ways deadlier than others. Since heartbreak and desire couldn't kill me on their own, I needed something—liquor, downers—that at least threatened my life a little bit.

I would likely have to retake the school year, but I postponed thoughts of the future. The whole program focused on *one day at a time*. Each morning I woke up and lived. In flashes, the euphoria of tequila sliding down my throat sometimes struck me, or I recalled a white pill on my tongue bringing me a gentle buzz, making me feel like a dragonfly. Sometimes my fight with my mom played in my mind like a movie. Even if I willed it to stop, it would continue in slow-motion slices, and I learned how to sit through it, to accept it. I let it all pass through me, hoping that, after reliving it enough times, the past would one day disintegrate, leave me alone for good before I'd make more mistakes that would haunt me.

At a certain point, I became enamored with seltzer waters, their crisp taste, the smooth texture of the can in my hands, the feeling of chugging. Women and men were separated into different sections, but we all mingled by the pool, and I tried not to glance at exposed skin, especially not the pale arms covered with dark tattoos. If I let myself approach them, it was only to request a cigarette, and they always complied. As the day darkened into night, I felt that familiar thrill, but I only remained sitting by the pool before it was curfew, and I had to go back inside and sleep and dream. Dreams of getting lost in the desert, of crawling in the sand on all fours like an animal, of barely surviving.

Then Diego was admitted. He gave me all the cigarettes I wanted, inserting them between my lips, igniting the flame for me. It was foreplay for when he would sneak into my room and finally be the one to undo me from the inside out. I felt slimy and renewed. Afterward, he whispered stories of shooting up heroin, of selling his car and computer and stealing cash from the register at his gas station job, of leaving cities only to return to his addiction. A few days later, he checked himself out, on the look for somewhere new to restart his lethal lust. A hickey on my collarbone kept him with me, if only for a little while.

After enough time passed, Vivian began calling. We never discussed what had been said; instead, we resumed to normal. She was always armed with updates. She heard rumors that Simon crashed his car on his way to Vegas and died on impact, tens of thousands of dollars burned to ashes in the backseat. Dave was in the hospital after doing acid and jumping off his girlfriend's roof—apparently he had a girlfriend the whole time. I finally explained what happened with Otto, and we reimagined his life in his cell. He was our puppet, our plaything, until one day I got a call from his wife.

I was in my room, flipping through the radio stations until I caught the end of a Leonard Cohen ballad. A staff member knocked on my door and said someone was on the phone for me. I thought it was Vivian, so I skipped along the beige tiles on my way to pick it up. I held the phone to my ear and my eyes widened and became unfocused. She had prepared a speech for me, and she spoke in a brisk flow without any breaks, relaying all of the bad things Otto had done, why he knew he deserved to be in prison, why he should never be let out, why I needed to stop sending him letters. I felt the warm tears slide down my cheeks, knowing he had been receiving them but never replied to a single one. Before she was finished, I hung up the phone. Over and over, her voice repeated in my head: *Otto is a bad, bad man*, but I couldn't believe it. My body was rejecting this simple truth. In my heart, Otto could do no wrong. I wouldn't permit it. We would live forever in that ephemeral kiss by the water, in his holding back my hair as I puked on the sidewalk, in our cosmic gaze at the gas station. Otto was mine to hold sacred in my memory, where I invented new scenes. I tore out a page from my notebook and began writing. *Dear Otto, in a perfect world, your mouth is on my knee, yellowed teeth sinking into flesh, not creating a hickey but instead eating me alive.*

filthyloot.com
@talentedperverts // @filthyloot

TALENTED PERVERTS™ is an imprint of Filthy Loot, focusing on "aesthetic fic
poetry, and art.

- ☐ *Microplastique* by Various
- ☐ *Latex, Texas* by Shane Jesse Christmass
- ☐ *Anxiety* by Various
- ☐ *Endless Now* by Ira Rat
- ☐ *I Rot* by Lana Valdez
- ☐ *Latex, Texas* by Shane Jesse Christmass
- ☐ *Letters to Jenny Just After She Died* by Charlene Elsby ‡
- ☐ *Little Birds* by Various
- ☐ *Little Birds (green)* by Various
- ☐ *Meth–DTF.* by Shane Jesse Christmass
- ☐ *Scandals* by Alex Osman
- ☐ *The Medication* by Ira Rat ‡

‡ Titles are limited e

www.ingramcontent.com/pod-product-compliance
Lightning Source LLC
LaVergne TN
LVHW092054060526
838201LV00047B/1387